Sherlock Holmes and

The Discarded Cigarette

As related from the case notes of

Dr. John H. Watson M.D.

Fred Thursfield

Paperback ISBN 9781780921174
ePub ISBN 9781780921181
PDF ISBN '9781780921198

Published in the UK by MX Publishing
335 Princess Park Manor, Royal Drive, London, N11 3GX
www.mxpublishing.com

Cover design by
www.staunch.com

Chapter 1

London, September 1895

It had been raining almost steadily for most of the month of September, the atmosphere this inclement weather had created in the city was a cold gray and damp one, these were the kinds of conditions that made you go about your daily business quickly if you were forced to be out of doors for any length of time or made you stay indoors with a warm coal fire in the hearth if you didn't need to be.

I hadn't really taken much notice of the weather myself what between attending to my morning rounds at St. Bartholomew's hospital, seeing patients in my surgery during the afternoon then home to spend the evening with my wife Mary. About the only time I ever noticed the miserable conditions at all was while I was stepping in and out of hansom cabs on my way to or from daily appointments.

The only person I was worried about the most during this time of year was my friend Holmes who unless he had a case to unravel, a problem that needed to be solved or some scientific experiment to conduct that would further add to his knowledge of crime I could imagine him pacing about in his rooms at 221B Baker street like some trapped animal looking for a way out.

Of course Holmes always had a "solution" (as he called it) to this problem which he kept safely locked in his desk drawer, I only hoped that a case worthy of his talents would come to him soon via some messenger or that I might have a cause to visit with him thus keeping "the solution" safely locked away where it was.

For years I had gradually weaned him from his habit which had threatened more than once to check his remarkable career now I knew that under ordinary conditions he no longer craved for this artificial stimulus, but I was well aware that the fiend was not dead, but only sleeping.

A reason for visiting my friend after a long absence presented its self a few days later when one evening after dinner when my wife announced she had just received a letter in the morning post from her sister in Brighton inviting Mary to come for an extended visit.

Next morning before heading to St. Bartholomew's hospital to conduct my morning rounds I escorted my wife and her luggage to Paddington station in time for her to board the London to Brighton train that would take her to her waiting sister.

Waving a fond fare well while standing on the station platform next to her carriage I found myself surrounded by a small group of people waving good bye to their friends and loved ones. I marveled at and watched as the large black steam engine, with two short blasts of its whistle came to life and slowly started pulling the collection of passenger carriages away from the station and down the tracks that would eventually take it to its passengers to their final destination then I made my way to the hospital to start my day.

Chapter 2

After my hospital rounds in the morning and attending to my surgery in the afternoon I hurried back to my home to pack a bag containing a change of clothes, my shaving kit and my service revolver then stepped outside in hopes of hailing a handsome cab that would take me to my friend.

The reason for a medical doctor a medical doctor owning a service revolver (from my time as a physician in the British Army medical corps in Afghanistan), much less having the knowledge of how to use it might seem to be a bit of a contradiction but the phrase "Quickly Watson, get your service revolver!" rang through my head as I was packing. All too often Holmes and I had found ourselves facing some dangerous and unpredictable characters in the course of solving a crime and I wanted to be prepared.

Seeing a black handsome cab arrive shortly in front of our house through the large parlor window I picked up my bag, headed out the door locked it and then seated myself in the cab "Where to Gov?" came the cab drivers booming voice from behind and slightly over head of me.

I gave him Holmes address then settled into a long ride that would take me across London and temporarily back to my bachelor days. As I listened to the sounds of the horses hoofs, the hansom cab's wheels on the wet cobble stone street and watched as the rainy late afternoon city scenery passed in front of and beside me I hoped my visit with Holmes wasn't going to be only about reminiscing and keeping my friends spirits up, I was genuinely looking forward to some type of adventure.

Sometime later we made a final right hand turn and I was again heading up a familiar street. When we stopped in front of the house I had known as a bachelor for some time, I let myself with my bag in hand out of the cab, paid the fare then walked to the entrance.

When Holmes and I had roomed together from 1881 until 1890, I would always let myself in with my key thus saving Mrs. Hudson (the house keeper) the bother of opening the door and announcing to Holmes that I had arrived. But I was only a guest now; so I knocked politely on the front door to announce my presence.

"Coming, coming" I heard an older familiar female voice on the other side of the door acknowledging that she had heard my announcement. The door opened inward and there in the door way stood a face and a form I had never quite forgotten, "Dr. Watson what a pleasure to see you again" Mrs. Hudson said with a smile that looked both happy and relieved at the same time.

"It's good to see you again too Mrs. Hudson" I replied while trying to read her expression as I entered. Drawing me into the narrow front hall Mrs. Hudson closed the front door behind me and started to ask a question when we both heard the familiar booming voice of Holmes asking from the front door of his upstairs rooms as to who had just arrived.

"It's Doctor Watson" she answered in Holmes general direction Again from the front door of his rooms I heard "Watson it's been too long, and it looks like I will have the pleasure of your company for some time" "How did he know?" I started to ask myself then remembering I was holding my bag I answered "Mary has gone south to Brighton for a time to visit with her sister---Holmes and no doubt to take in the brisk sea air, this means until her timely return I have the pleasure of your company."

"You made an excellent choice of temporary residence then" Holmes replied, at this point he descended the carpeted stairs to where I could see him. For the reader who has not yet met my friend I will give you a brief description of him as he was facing me while standing on the bottom stair.

Starting from the feet he was wearing dark brown bed room slippers, he was dressed in black pressed trousers, a white dress shirt but no collar or tie, all of this was carried by a tall and somewhat angular frame.

His head was topped by jet black hair which was combed straight back, his deep dark hazel eyes, set in chiseled facial features had an almost unnerving ability to pierce through you to root out the truth and his somewhat thin lips passed only the occasional hint of a of what I always thought of as a bemused smile.

I would not describe Holmes at all a stuffy straight-laced Victorian gentleman; in fact, I would describe him and his habits as "Bohemian." He may alternate between days or weeks of listless lassitude and similar periods of intense engagement with a challenging case or with his hobby, experimental chemistry to keep his spirits up.

With a gracious sweep of his right hand in the general direction of his rooms he said invitingly "Well come up Watson and you can tell me of your latest adventures while I straighten up my parlor." "Brace yourself Doctor Watson" Mrs. Hudson said in a low voice as she made her way past me towards the pantry to prepare the afternoon tea.

Not quite sure what to make of her comment I climbed the carpeted stairs as I followed Holmes up to his rooms. His front door was open when I walked in behind him, as I entered his familiar parlor I now knew what Mrs. Hudson had meant by her cryptic comment; for the entire room was filled with the blue gray smoke of cigarettes and cigars seemingly burning everywhere

Chapter 3

As I entered Holmes parlor I exclaimed "Holmes it's a wonder that you can see or even breathe at all considering the amount cigarette and cigar smoke that is in this room right now." "It's worse in here than any gentleman's smoking room in London." Holmes turned and countered "Ah Watson, not a smoking room but an ongoing scientific experiment whereby I will be able to identify not only any brand of cigarette or cigar being smoked, but also its country of origin and where it was purchased. "

The over whelming smell I encountered was as if a large tobacco shop had caught fire and all of its merchandise was being consumed by the flames. Surveying the situation I saw ash trays of all sizes, colors and descriptions placed on almost every horizontal surfaces with in the room each holding burning tobacco products. I alarmingly asked Holmes "How can you breathe the air in here, how can you even see in here?" "It's all in the name of science Watson" he replied

I started to ask the obvious question as to why when Holmes put his hand up to stop me. "Think Watson at almost every crime scene what is the one most common thing that is seen but always overlooked by some minor detective of the Metropolitan Police because it seems almost too trivial or not worthy of any real attention?"

How often have we been looking for the obvious clues and witnessed only by chance a half smoked cigarette that might have been extinguished then carelessly tossed aside, possibly even by the perpetrator of the crime?"

"Realistically all this would tell us that the person was a smoker." I replied "More than that," Holmes continued as he picked up and examined a still smoldering cigarette "by analyzing both the paper and the tobacco of the discarded item we might discover its origins, where it had been purchased and possibly by whom, leading us another step closer to our suspect."

"Does this have anything to do with the dense fog of cigarette and cigar smoke I encountered when I entered your parlor just now?" "Yes, what I have been doing over the last several weeks is that I have been purchasing different brands of cigarettes and cigars available from various tobacconists here in London." Thinking to myself of what Mrs. Hudson had to endure during these scientific trials I listened as Holmes continued

With each one I would let it burn most of the way down, I would then extinguish it and commit to memory the brand, the tobacco it contained, the paper or leaf it was wrapped in, what it looked like and smelled like when I put it to my nose. To that I would add the already known information as to where it had been made, sold and who may have purchased it." As if to illustrate the point Holmes sniffed the still lit cigarette then returned it to its ashtray and extinguished it.

Still skeptical I asked "Do you mean that if you were to find an discarded cigarette in the cold and wet high street this afternoon you could tell where it had been had been made and sold and no less the identity of the smoker?"

Looking confident as always Holmes smiled slightly then gave me a qualified answer "If it was dry and among the ones I have already committed to memory so far, yes."

To my considerable relief it turned out that Holmes had taken a slightly less dangerous way to deal with his boredom. Finding the smoky air in his parlor harder to breathe by the minute I commented "If I don't get to breathe some fresh air in the next few minutes I shall pass out from all this thick tobacco haze."

Chapter 4

Then not waiting for any acknowledgment of my request or for my friend's approval I made my way to large parlor windows which faced onto Baker Street, raised each one up in turn and as I did, saw the warm blue gray cigarette and cigar smoke from the room escape out into the cold afternoon and smelled the rain dampened fresh air coming in.

While I was busy doing that Holmes started going about his parlor putting out the still lit and smoldering cigarettes and cigars. "Assist me in bringing this scientific experiment to an end Watson so that when Mrs. Hudson arrives with the afternoon tea there will be some place where we can sit and eat."

So between the two of us we extinguished and collected all the tobacco products and their containers, just as we were finding one convenient place to store them until after tea there was a knock at the door indicating that the meal had arrived. As she entered carrying the tray in bearing food and drink Mrs. Hudson gave the state of the room in general and Holmes both a disapproving a look.

Realizing he may have strained their relationship a little more than usual Holmes apologetically said to Mrs. Hudson "I apologize for the state of my rooms. After Doctor Watson and I have finished eating we will leave you to attend to the dishes while we both will attend" Holmes said with a general wave of his hand "to the rest."

With a slight hint of acknowledgment Mrs. Hudson placed the tray on Holmes dining table as she turned to leave the room muttered "Thank you Mr. Holmes." During tea I related what had been happening in my sedentary life, I told him of my comings and goings with my practice in the hospital and my day surgery and out of respect to Holmes bachelor status giving only the briefest description of my married life.

After I had finished Holmes replied "I wish Watson that I could enliven our conversation with tales of master criminals and well planned crimes, but alas I have only been called upon by the Metropolitan Police to solve how some petty criminal managed a minor break and entry, hardly worthy of an entry in your journal." I must explain here that I consider myself to be both a friend of Holmes as well as his chronicler (his "Boswell").

Most of Holmes' stories are told as narratives, his solutions to actual crimes. In some later stories, Holmes criticizes me for my writings, usually because I relate them as exciting stories rather than as objective and detailed reports focusing on what Holmes regards as the pure "science" of Holmes' craft.

Well, I thought to myself my time with Holmes will be quiet and unexciting and that I would be counting the days until my wife's return. "I believe" my friend said he put his napkin down, rose from the dining table and walked towards the still open parlor windows "It's as if Watson all the criminals of London have taken a vacation from crime and gone abroad to the continent for the sun."

Chapter 5

After his rooms had been made respectable and the dishes from the tea removed Holmes said that he had an appointment with the Metropolitan Police about a possible forged oil painting "And they asked me if I could apply my limited knowledge of art to assist them to prove if it was or wasn't" was how Holmes finished.

"And you Watson?" He asked as he made his way towards where his over coat and top hat were hanging I told him I was going to spend the rest of the day here in his rooms updating my notes. "Ah yes your journal" he quipped hoping that I wasn't writing as we were talking.

While he was putting on his outer ware to go out and as I was reaching into my left breast pocket for the pouch containing tobacco for my pipe I suddenly remembered the two lecture tickets that had been given to me a previous morning by one of my patients because finding himself in hospital he was now unable to attend.

As I pulled them out from my vest pocket I queried my friend as I saw him heading for the front door "Holmes, did we have any plans for tomorrow evening?" Stopping momentarily he turned in my direction and replied "Other than spending an evening scouring the papers for some hint of a crime that may have been committed; no I don't believe we have any. Why do you ask?"

While looking at the tickets I answered "Well I was given a pair of tickets by a patient of mine for a lecture that is to be given at the St. James's Theater in King Street tomorrow evening." sensing that I now had aroused his curiosity Holmes asked with some interest "And who is the lecturer?" "An H.G. Wells" I answered "and he will be speaking about a new book he has just had published."

Holmes pondered my reply for a moment "H.G. Wells let me think; yes I believe he is a novelist, journalist, sociologist, historian and a member of the Fabian Society if I am correct."

I must pause here to acquaint the reader with the society to which Holmes had just mentioned. The Fabian Society is a British socialist intellectual movement, whose purpose is to advance the socialist cause by reformist, rather than revolutionary, means.

"An excellent suggestion" Holmes continued "what time does this lecture begin?" I turned the tickets over to see when the performance was scheduled to begin "8:00 o'clock it says" " Then Watson I shall make the necessary arrangements with the hansom cab driver who will be taking me to my destination this evening to arrange that we have transportation waiting for us at 7:00 o'clock tomorrow evening giving us enough time to arrive at the theater."

With that Holmes was dressed and out the door and onto his evening errand. Once the over powering smell of smoked cigarettes and cigars had finally left the room I pulled down each of the large parlor windows to keep the damp and cold outside, I stoked the coal fire in the hearth, lit the coal oil lamp on the small table beside me and my pipe then comfortably settled in the large green leather chair next to the table to continue with my journal.

Chapter 6

I heard Holmes downstairs letting himself in the front door just as the mantle clock was chiming 10 p.m. As he was coming through the front door of his rooms I looked up from my writing and asked him with some interest if he had any luck with the forgery.

"Due to the obvious quality of the painting Watson, the Metropolitan Police and myself agree we lack the necessary artistic skills to discern if it is a forgery or not. To this end it is to being taken to the Belgravia Gallery tomorrow morning where their experts in forgery will ascertain if it is or is not. "

After removing and hanging up his over coat and top hat he sat down in his favorite chair for a minute to scan the evening newspapers looking over the top of the news paper he had in his hands Holmes asked in passing "speaking of tomorrow night's lecture do you know the title of this new novel written by Mr. H.G. Wells?"

"The Time Machine, I believe" I answered some what quietly while waiting for some sort of predictable and skeptical reaction from Holmes. Holmes thought for a moment, and then he said something very unpredictable "

"A machine that travels through time in the hands of a master criminal, Watson what an interesting if somewhat a disturbing thought. The nature and types of crime that could be committed are astounding. " "Is there anything of interest in the news paper?" I asked him after a short time to get him away from thinking more about time machines in the hands of criminals.

He was aware that by anything of interest, I had meant anything of criminal interest. There was the news of a revolution, of a possible war, and of an impending change of government; but these did not come within the horizon of my companion. I could see nothing recorded in the shape of crime which was not commonplace and futile. Holmes groaned and resumed his restless meanderings.

The London criminal is certainly a dull fellow," Holmes said in the querulous voice of the sportsman whose game has failed him. "Look out of these windows this evening Watson." Holmes indicated to his windows facing onto Baker Street

"See how the figures loom up, are dimly seen, and then blend once more into the cloudbank. The thief or the murderer could roam London on such a day as the tiger does the jungle, unseen until he pounces, and then evident only to his victim."

"There have," he said, "been numerous petty thefts." Holmes snorted his contempt as he folded up the paper and dropped it by his side. "This great and somber stage is set for something more worthy than that," said he. "It is fortunate for this community that I am not a criminal." "It is, indeed!" said I heartily.

Chapter 7

As it had been arranged by Holmes the previous evening, precisely at 7:00 o'clock our transport was waiting in the street for us. As I climbed in, Holmes gave the driver our destination then climbed in beside me. With quick jerk of the horse's reins we were off traveling the nighttime gas lit still wet cobble stone streets of London.

After traveling across the city for some time we found ourselves on King Street and only a few of blocks away from our final destination. As our hansom slowly cab pulled up to the well gas lit front entrance of the theater both Holmes and I could tell by the number of people mingling about outside St. James's and waiting to enter that many others in London were as curious to find out about this new author as we were.

After Holmes paid the fare we left the cab and proceeded inside, we then made our way from the busy and bustling front entrance of the theater, checked our coats and hats, had our tickets verified by an usher then Holmes and I made our way through small and large groups of people engaged in conversation.

We crossed the ornately decorated and carpeted chandelier lit foyer and found our way into semi darkened theater where we looked for the row letter and seat numbers that had been stamped on our tickets. "Here we are Watson, row E seats 20 and 21 and it appears that our seats are located about mid way along the row."

Finally making our way to our seats with out any one impeding our progress Holmes and I settled in to our respective seats and waited for the performance to begin. As we were sitting there together I soaked up the atmosphere and conversations that was going on all around me. Holmes was scanning the audience I assumed looking to locate some of the missing criminal element he had commented on earlier.

Before either of us had any time to really take in the people sitting beside us and in front of us the gas lights on the walls of the theater were being dimmed. At the same time two stage hands were crossing the large stage from right to left lighting in turn each of the lime lights that would illuminate the performer.

As the last of the theaters gas lights were being extinguished the level of conversation also seemed to be extinguished too. When the theater was quiet a tall distinguished looking gentleman in formal evening dress appeared from the right wing of the stage (obviously the master of ceremonies), when he reached the middle of the stage he stopped, turned and faced the audience.

"Good evening ladies and gentlemen," he said in a deep booming male voice that I'm sure could be heard all the way to the exits at the back of the theater "on behalf of the St. James Theater and our guest speaker I would like to thank you for coming to hear him this evening".

There was a pause "Mr. H.G. Wells is known to many in London as a novelist, journalist, sociologist, and historian. Tonight he comes to us as a writer of a new form of prose, which he calls science fiction."

The novel he will be reading excerpts from tonight is his first one to be written and published in this new style. Mr. Wells will read a few short passages from his novel then if there is time after he will take questions from the audience.

The master of ceremonies paused again for a moment the continued "Following this evening's performance Mr. Wells will be available in the St. James's Theater foyer for a short time after to sign copies of his new book if any one has already purchased one and wishes to have it autographed by the author

"And now ladies and gentlemen with out further delay I give you this evening's performer Mr. H.G. Wells."

With that the applause from the audience started slowly then continued to build. As the applause continued the master of ceremonies returned to the right wing of the stage as he did he was passed by who everybody in the audience assumed to be H.G. Wells. Wells appearance was quite different; he was short, young looking (I would have placed his age at around 29), he had a full head of auburn hair, with a slightly drooping mustache of the same color and he had what some would call melancholy looking eyes.

Where the master of ceremonies had been formally attired Wells wore what might be considered an everyday tan colored woolen business suit with white shirt, collar and dark colored tie, to finish he was wearing what some might call "walking shoes". In his left hand he was carrying a blue leather bound book, the book we assumed he was going to be reading from.

Wells now stood in the same place where the master of ceremonies had a few moments ago "Good evening ladies and gentlemen," Wells started then realized with his voice he could not compete with the applause waited for it to die down and finish then continued "my name is Herbert George Wells and I will be reading some short passages from my new novel The Time Machine also known as The Chronic Argonauts."

He opened up his book to the page that had been book marked looked down and began reading. At this point I will not bore the reader with the word for word context of all the passages that were read on the stage that evening, but there were three passages of particular interest that caught both Holmes and my attention.

This little affair,' said the Time Traveler, resting his elbows upon the table and pressing his hands together above the apparatus, 'is only a model. It is my plan for a machine to travel through time.

You mean to say that machine (the model) has traveled into the future?' said Filby. 'Into the future or the past - I don't, for certain, know which.' After an interval the Psychologist had an inspiration. 'It must have gone into the past if it has gone anywhere,' he said. 'Why?' said the Time Traveler.

'Because I presume that it has not moved in space, and if it traveled into the future it would still be here all this time, since it must have traveled through this time.' 'But,' I said, 'If it traveled into the past it would have been visible when we came first into this room; and last Thursday when we were here; and the Thursday before that; and so forth!' (H.G. Wells the Time machine)

Chapter 8

As it turns out there was another person in the audience of the St. James that evening that had more than a passing literary interest in the science fiction writings of Wells than either Holmes or I did. "Watson" Holmes said in a low voice as he leaned in my direction "You know it's not usually in my nature to give in to premonitions but I think we should have a word with author after, perhaps while he is occupied with autographing copies of his book."

"What makes you think like this?" I questioned "I thought I saw the back of a familiar form two rows ahead of us" was Holmes answer "and if it is who I think it is I cannot help but think he is not here solely for the sake of literature".

He then instructed me "When Mr. Wells is finished Watson, proceed from your seat to the foyer and secure a place in book signing queue for both of us before too many more people from the audience are ahead of us." "While you are doing this I am going to see if the form I saw belongs to the man I think he might be."

As H.G. Wells was taking his second curtain call to an almost standing ovation, I made my way quickly from the theater to the foyer to see that there were only a few people were lined up in the book signing queue for the author to arrive. As instructed I got into the queue, as I was waiting a gentleman two people ahead of me caught my attention.

Even from where I was standing I noticed right away he was half a head taller than myself; I thought him a bit on the thin side, he had dark sparse hair and was well dressed, which indicated to me that he might be gainfully employed. The one thing that kept my attention on him was an air of nervous energy that seemed to be about him. As if he had a burning question that required an immediate answer from the author.

The sound of approaching applause, which momentarily broke my concentration, indicated that Wells had entered the theater foyer After the author had seated himself at the desk and chair that the theater had been provided for him the book signing queue slowly began to move forward, I looked around and did not notice Holmes any where, so instead of introducing Holmes to the author as I had planned to I could only introduce myself and relate to Wells, I only hoped correctly was that Holmes had enjoyed the reading.

Before I knew it the man with the air of nervous energy about him was standing in front of H.G. Wells I was close enough to catch most to the conversation that passed between them. "Mr. Wells" the man started "I regret not having a copy of your book for you to autograph, but be assured I will be purchasing a copy first thing tomorrow. I do have one question for you though, is the time machine in your story a possibility?"

"Mr." Wells paused while he waited to hear his questioner's last name "Druitt sir Montague John Druitt" was the questioners answer. "Mr. Druitt let me assure you that the machine in my book is a work of pure fiction and imagination only."

"During the last part of the 19th century we have witnessed the invention of great marvels of technology but we do not at this time possess the knowledge or even the ability to create such a machine that could propel a man as far forward in time as I have suggested."

When Druitt, no doubt a little disappointed at the answer he received and the person behind him departed it was my turn to speak to the author. I first introduced myself and then apologized for Holmes absence.

"I can assure you Mr. Wells if my friend were here he would compliment you on your story and in the manner it was written," "When you see him next thank him for me" was Wells response then he continued "I must ask if you are the same Doctor Watson who writes for the Strand chronicling the cases of Mr. Sherlock Holmes."

Surprised and a little bit flattered at the question I replied "Yes I am, although if my friend were present he would tell you that I relate them as exciting stories rather than as objective and detailed reports focusing on what Holmes regards as the pure "science".

Then remembering my conversation with Holmes about the time machine earlier in the theater, I asked if Welles was free some after noon to meet with Holmes and myself to discuss his book in greater detail.

"The pleasure would be mine Doctor Watson" was Wells response to my request. Giving him a card with Holmes address on it I said my farewells and set off looking to see if I could locate Holmes in the now fairly crowded and bustling theater foyer After searching for a short time and having no luck in locating him I finally retrieved my coat and hat and made my way towards the well lit entrance of the theater and King Street in hopes of attracting a hansom cabbies attention for transport back to 221 B Baker Street.

Then as if by some magicians trick I suddenly heard my name in the night air "Watson!" and there was Holmes already seated in one waiting for me. "Holmes you never cease to surprise me." I said as I climbed in. "Did you locate the person you were looking for?" I asked. "No" Holmes replied to my question "He must have melted into the large body of people who had gathered in the theater foyer after Mr. Well's performance.

"I trust although you were able to talk with the author for a few minutes?" " Holmes queried. I told him I had and that I had invited Wells to Holmes room's tomorrow afternoon to talk more about his book.

As the hansom cab pulled away into the night I related "I must tell you that while I was waiting in the queue I saw a man who caught my attention and while he was talking to H.G. Wells I happen to overhear his name, it sounded some what familiar and I wondered if you might remember it" I said "The name of this man?" Holmes questioned "John Druitt" I replied

Holmes then asked me to give a physical description of Druitt, and it turned out to be the very man Holmes had been seeking earlier in the theater "ah yes Montague John Druitt," Holmes closed his eyes to remember "originally from Dorset I believe, he was a graduate of Winchester College and an avid sportsman.

I believe Druitt was considered by many to be the number one suspect in the Jack the Ripper case. Interestingly enough, there was very little evidence with which to implicate his him. I also remember that he had been incarcerated for the theft of small to medium sized oil paintings and was also in the business of creating reasonably good forgeries of the stolen paintings to sell to less than discriminate buyers."

Chapter 9

The next day proved to be far brighter for myself and Holmes in that the weather had much improved and in the much anticipated visit of a famous author. "Mr. Holmes, Doctor Watson a Mr. Wells is here to see you" came the familiar voice of Mrs. Hudson from the downstairs inside front entrance of the house.

"Send him up please Mrs. Hudson" Holmes raised his voice loud enough so that he did not have to immediately get up from the chair where he was seated. Shortly after the person who we had both seen on stage the night before came through the front door of Holmes rooms. Both Homes and I got up walked towards our visitor and welcomed him. "The pleasure is all mine gentlemen" Wells replied in return "it is an honor to be in the company of two famous persons as yourselves."

While removing his coat and hat Wells complimented Holmes by saying "I feel as if I already know you Mr. Holmes from Doctor Watson's chronicles in the Strand" "Mr. Wells" Holmes countered "I must tell you that Watson does have a tendency to magnify the few skills and abilities I put to use when solving a case. Since I rarely if ever get to read his notes before he has them published I can only imagine that the account of both the crime and criminal are far more interesting on paper then they ever were while I was dealing with either."

As all three of us sat down, Mrs. Hudson came in bearing a silver tray on it was a pot of freshly brewed tea, cups, saucers, spoons, cream and sugar. After tea was served all around Mrs. Hudson left the room and Holmes started "I must compliment on your performance at the St. James Theater the other night Mr. Wells, I would have done so in person but there was a gentlemen in the audience that I had wished to talk with."

Holmes then asked Wells to give an outline of his story. Wells went on to tell Holmes about the inventor and his machine, where the inventor went in time and the consequences of his travels. "It would seem to be an awesome responsibility to own such a machine then" Holmes commented after. "A lot of good could be done with it as well as a lot of harm."

Then again to assure himself as well as me Holmes commented to Wells almost as if a question "It is good to know that such a machine is purely a work of only fiction and imagination then." With that observation Wells looked like he wanted to share some dark secret because he paused before answering "I have not been entirely truthful with my readers and both of you on that matter."

Holmes interest was piqued with Wells surprising statement and while looking directly at him Holmes queried "How so?" Wells looking almost relieved to share his secret replied

"I have long thought that it might be possible, in theory at least to have a set of mechanical drawings that could again in theory describe how to build my time machine. Gentlemen the machine in my story is now one step beyond fiction, theory and imagination. I now own a set of mechanical drawings, that with the right materials, skills and abilities it could be built."

As if some how to sort this out Holmes commented "Mr. Wells do you realize that if you were to reveal to any one on the high street what you have just shared with Dr. Watson and myself they would say that the venture is impossible and that you have temporarily taken leave of your senses." Wells countered Holmes statement with "Mr. Holmes I have always believed that the only way to achieve the impossible is to believe it is possible."

I had rarely seen Holmes at a loss for words no matter how shocking the revelation, but with Wells unexpected news and unshakable conviction this was one of those times. Holmes quickly recovered from the impact with two short questions

"Mr. Wells to assure myself I must ask you" Holmes started "first that the machine could (Holmes emphasized the word could) be built but cannot be built at this time and second that the mechanical drawings you speak of are safely under lock and key at all times?"

With a silent nod of his head Wells indicated yes to both questions. "There we have it then" Holmes stated with a sigh of relief in his voice "I would suggest that you do not share this particular part of your work with anyone. Then changing direction Holmes asked "Is there anyone other than you, Watson and myself that have any knowledge of these drawings?"

"No, Mr. Holmes and with the present state of affairs with my ex-wife she has no knowledge of the drawings much less where they are kept." To end any further discussion of Wells marital state Holmes finished the conversation with "Well then all of London can rest assured that nobody will be going forward in time to see what the city might look like in say one hundred years time."

Chapter 10

I would not have made any mention about the state of Wells marriage in 1891 to Isabel Mary Wells his cousin at all, but as events were about to unfold it would later play an important part in the case During his marriage to Isabel, Wells had liaisons with a number of women, including the American birth control activist Margaret Sanger but left Isabel in 1894 for one of his students, Amy Catherine Robbins, whom he married late in 1895.

From information gathered later it was said that the first Mrs. Wells had been less than pleased with these circumstances when she found out about the extra martial affairs her husband was carrying on while he was still married to her. The eventual revenge the first Mrs. Wells had planned against her husband would have ramifications that she could never have thought possible. Holmes would quote towards the end of this case "Hell hath no fury, like a women scorned."

Of course this wasn't the first time Holmes and I encountered mechanical drawings or plans that could have great ramifications if they were to fall into the wrong hands.

There were the Bruce Partington plans. Holmes's brother Mycroft had come to London about some missing, secret submarine plans. Seven of the ten pages - three are still missing - were found with Arthur Cadogan West's body. He was a young clerk in a government office at Royal Arsenal, Woolwich, whose body was found next to the Underground tracks near Aldgate, his head crushed.

He had little money with him (although there appears to have been no robbery), theatre tickets, and curiously, no Underground ticket. The three missing pages by themselves could enable one of Britain's enemies to build a Bruce-Partington submarine.

Some of the last words Wells spoke to us that afternoon just before the end of his visit would in their own way be prophetic. Wells had not realized at the time of course that his first wife had through knowledge passed from a household maid who on at least two occasions seen him Wells, without his knowing place the large bundle of rolled mechanical drawings of the time machine into a sturdy metal strong box and then lock it.

When the maid had asked about the nature of contents of the strong box Wells had given her a rather dismissive answer saying only that they had only something to do with a story he was writing. The first Mrs. Wells with this knowledge now had her curiosity mixed with a possible way to seek revenge for the embarrassment and shame she felt that her husband had brought onto her.

When the tea pot was empty Wells rose from where he had been seated and said "Well gentlemen I must take my leave. I have return home and prepare for an extensive lecture tour I am about to embark on."

Holmes momentarily sensing some unknown danger asked "Where is your lecture to take place and how long will you be away from London Mr. Wells?" "The East Midlands Mr. Holmes my first stop will be Northampton, and then on to Leicester, Nottingham then my last stop is in Derby."

"Travelling by rail between engagements I should think no more than about a week; it seems my books popularity has preceded its author."Wells cheerily replied as he stood up to retrieve his coat and hat.

Holmes, to ease his feeling of foreboding then asked "I assume that the only key to the strong box containing the mechanical drawings of your time machine will be in your possession at all times?' Wells smiled as he pulled out his watch fob chain; there on the end of the chain was the only key that Wells assuredly knew about.

Chapter 11

At this time I must shift the readers focus away from 221B Baker Street to 12 Fitzroy Road, Primrose Hill (also in London) being the residence of H.G. Wells and his former first wife Isabel Mary Wells.

The atmosphere during the last part of the marriage in the house time could be described as frosty each being cordial with each other but you could tell that there was a chasm between the two that would never be bridged again. Whenever Wells returned to his residence he must have thought "A man always finds it hard to realize that he may have finally lost a woman's love, however badly he may have treated her."

When the same maid, via a messenger alerted the former Mrs. Wells of her ex husbands speaking tour she knew it was time to put her plan into action. When Isabel Mary Wells arrived the next day at 12 Fitzroy Road, Primrose Hill (also in London) again being the residence of H.G. Wells she asked the maid in person where the strong box was located and how long would her ex husband be away for.

Having some time ago made a wax impression of the key, and now being in possession of a duplicate key for the lock on the strong box she had ready access to the contents inside.

Knowing that Wells was now safely away from the city, her first act was to open up the strong box and see if the contents might have some immediate monetary value. Unlocking and opening up the strong box she took the large heavy roll out of the box and placed it on her ex husband's desk she unrolled it from right to left to see the title page of the large thick document read

"A Theoretical Machine to Travel Back and Forward Through Time". Below the title read "These mechanical drawings have been commissioned under the direction of Mr. Herbert George Wells and have been drawn by James B. Francis Chief Engineer for the Proprietors of Locks and Kirk Boott agent of the Merrimack Manufacturing Company 1894"

As she stood looking at page after page of meticulous mechanical drawings each outlining how the individual parts of the time machine along with its various controls were to be manufactured, how all of it was to be assembled allowing the operator to go anywhere they wanted in time the first Mrs. Wells was in momentary awe of her ex husband's creativity.

But knowing that she had only a short time until her husband's return she would have to find a way to make copy of the mechanical drawings for her own use then return the originals to the strong box. Through her husband's publisher she located the firm of Bolliger & Mabillard Consulting Engineers which was located at 15 Holllybush Lane Penn Wolverhampton, London.

With a note that appeared to had been written and signed by her husband stating that he (Wells) required the firm to reproduce a second set of mechanical drawings of the time machine and the original drawings now momentarily in her procession the first Mrs. Wells put her plan into action.

Chapter 12

It is one thing to own (no matter by what means it was obtained) something that might be unique and possibly valuable it is another thing to find a ready market or a buyer to sell it to. This was the short term problem the first Mrs. Well faced when she returned to Bolliger & Mabillard to pick up the original mechanical drawings plus the copy.

The exact details as to how the first Mrs. Wells solved this problem may never be known but the solution to her sale of and how Montague John Druitt became involved in the purchase of the mechanical drawings came together in a place or a district named The Rookery.

The worst sink of iniquity was The Rookery, a place or rather district, so named, whose shape was triangular, bounded by Bainbridge Street, George Street and High Street, St Giles. The colony, called The Rookery, was like a honeycomb, perforated by a number of courts and blind alleys, cul de sac, without any outlet other than the entrance. Here was the lowest lodging houses in London, inhabited by the various classes of thieves common to large cities were banded together.

It was thought that the name of the district may have come from the slang expression *to rook* that is to cheat or steal, a verb well established in the 16th century and associated with the supposedly thieving nature of the rook bird.

Montague John Druitt's residence and where he conducted his criminal activities from was located at upstairs lodging rooms in the Old Mint, along the Ratcliffe Highway and Petticoat Lane in the Rookery.

It was here that the copy of the mechanical drawings of H.G. Well's time machine was exchanged for a large sum of money. Thinking that she had damaged her husband's reputation and had received a fair financial compensation for the shame she had to endure as a result of her husband's affair Isabel Mary Wells left Druitt's residence thinking nothing more about the transaction.

They say that sometimes the right elements can come together at the right time and produce great good or great evil. In the case of Druitt's purchase the latter would prove to be true and would test my friend's criminal deduction talents to their limit.

With his long sought after prize in hand Montague John Druitt was to take leave of his residence in the Rookery and the City of London shortly for trip abroad to the continent. While booking passage on the Cherbourg, a Cunard Steamship Company vessel that would take him across the English Channel to France he also booked railway passage to two cities in Europe.

His first stop would be Baden Muehlburg, Germany to meet with Gotlieb Daimler and Karl Friedrich Benz who together at their machine works would manufacture the frame and the mechanical workings of the time machine, then onto Smiljan Lika, Croatia to meet with Nikola Tesla who at his laboratory would create the necessary intricate electrical dials and controls that would allow the time machines operator to go forwards and backwards in time.

After agreeing as to payment for services tendered from the three inventors, the completed components from Daimler, Benz and Tesla were to be disassembled then packed into large wooden shipping crates that would be transported from the continent to an address located at the junction of Garrett Lane and Summers town Road in Camden town London. Of course at the time we were not in possession of this information but would learn of Druitt's itinerary later.

Chapter 13

I bring the reader's attention back again to 221 B Baker Street and a conversation Holmes and I had concerning an art forgery *"Due to the obvious quality of the painting"* Holmes had said *"the Metropolitan Police and myself agree we lack the necessary artistic skills to discern if it is a forgery or not. To this end it is to being taken to the Belgravia Gallery tomorrow morning where their experts in forgery will decide if it is or isn't."*

And it was only a short time after Wells had returned from his lecture tour in the East Midlands that Holmes and I would be making the first of several visits to the Belgravia Gallery located at 45 Albemarle Street, Mayfair London in connection to forged paintings.

Holmes had of course known of the Gallery through its reputation of over 30 years of European trained expertise to all paintings that are in need of cleaning, repair, conservation, or major restoration. Their philosophy was to alter the artwork as little as possible with respect to the original intention of the artist. To that end, they examined each work of art closely and tailored their methodologies to its' precise needs.

Paintings were very rarely lined; rather were re-woven or in some cases inlay canvas and use a bridge technique to affix it to the original canvas. They used only the finest materials and techniques, which are found in major museums around the world. In accordance with their belief that restoration should be noninvasive, all of the work they did is fully reversible.

The Belgravia Gallery worked with and is especially proud of its ongoing relationship with national museums, universities, art galleries, art dealers, and private clients.

As we were getting out of the hansom cab in front in front of the gallery I was impressed by its architectural design. The building was covered in polished gray marble stone on the left was a large display window trimmed in brass displaying some contemporary paintings, in the middle was the entrance and to the right was a display window of the same size as the one on the left it too was trimmed in brass and was also displaying contemporary paintings

As Holmes and I made our way through the brass trimmed entrance of the gallery I asked "What is the name of the painting we have come to examine?" "The Long Engagement by Arthur Hughes and I believe it was painted in 1859" was his answer. Once inside the foyer just as the gallery manager was approaching us Holmes finished his description with "and it was on loan from the Birmingham Art Gallery when this incident took place." Mr. Holmes, Dr. Watson I presume" queried the distinguished looking gallery manager as he extended his right hand in Holmes direction. "Yes" was Holmes reply to the query…"My name is Charles Henry Stephenson and I am the managing director of the Belgravia Gallery" "and you have obviously come about the Hughes painting."

If you would both come with me to the restoration work shop area I think what we may have accidently uncovered something that might be of some interest to you both." As Holmes and I walked through the gallery I was impressed by the decor of the gallery and its range and scope of paintings that were mounted on the walls waiting to be viewed by and bought by potential collectors.

Passing through a set of plain wooden double hinged doors that divided the gallery from upper class to working class we first noticed the mixed smells of oil paint and turpentine. Holmes and I now saw a scene all around us of various sizes of paintings some on easels covered with a cloth to protect them while they dried, some being worked on by what I took to be expert craftsmen in their trade. Other uncovered paintings of various sizes were leaning with their backs against the walls of the large work space each waiting their turn for repair or restoration.

There was one covered painting that had been set aside from the others which I took to be that painting we had come to see. "Excuse me Mr. Holmes and Dr. Watson while I get the young man who started working on the Hughes and I can have him better explain to you what he has discovered" the director said as he went further into the restoration area seeking one particular person.

He returned shortly with a young man of medium build, probably in his mid twenties who looked like and dressed some what that he might have been an old master himself in another life time. "Mr. Holmes Dr. Watson this is Jeffery Daniels one of our art restorers." Before the introductions could be properly completed and the painting properly reveled Holmes started.

"Mr. Daniels before you begin, I must ask have you started or completed any restoration work on any other paintings by Arthur Hughes." "Why would you ask that?" I queried "To be certain that Mr. Daniels is familiar with the style the artist employs, his choice of oil colors, the manufacturer of the paint the artist prefers, his particular brush strokes and even Hughes choice of canvas " Holmes replied knowledgeably.

Chapter 14

Jeffery Daniels taking this line of questioning in stride proceeded to display his knowledge of the painter by stating that Hughes was a pre-Raphaelite painter and book illustrator then went on to list Orlando, Home From the Sea and April Love among the particular artists paintings he had worked on.

With that the young art restorer lifted the cloth covering the "The Long Engagement" the true nature of the painting sitting on the wooden easel was about to be revealed. For the reader not familiar with this particular work of Arthur Hughes I will briefly describe the painting that was resting on the easel before us.

It was a work of modest size and painted in the portrait style, to the left of the viewer there was the large trunk of poplar tree in a meadow setting, leaning against the tree was a red headed young man dressed in what is called the country style.

To his right standing beside him, limply holding his hand was a red headed young lady also dressed in the country style. I had always assumed that the title of the painting had been drawn from the forlorn looks on each of the young lover's faces.

Young Daniels gave us all a couple of minutes to observe the painting then proceeded to tell us why he felt it might be a forgery. He started "When I started the restoration work, meaning to clean the accumulated dust away that any painting acquires when it has hung for some time I started to think that cobalt violet in the young ladies cloak didn't seem quite right."

The same went for the cadmium red light in her hair lastly the chromium oxide green used in the moss at the base of tree wasn't right. I have it on good authority that the artist used Gamblin Oils when painting The Long Engagement and the ones used for this particular painting are not.

"Of course the further along I got I thought that the whole Hughes looked some how different I then consulted our copy of the Brice Art Museum Exhibition Catalog 1890 edition (which was sitting on a work table near to Holmes) right away to check, the color plate of the particular Hughes painting you are looking for Mr. Holmes is on page 52. "

As Holmes picked up and thumbed through the catalog that he had been made aware of he located the particular color plate young Daniels had pointed out. "As you can see, even to the untrained eye there are obvious differences between what is shown in the catalog and what you see before you."

"What you are looking at Mr. Holmes is indeed at best a very clever forgery, when viewed from the distance the public is made to stand back from any painting in any art gallery it could easily appear to be and be passed off as an original, however when you are able to examine it from the distance you are at now at then you can tell that it is not."

Chapter 15

I leave the revelations of the forged oil painting for a moment to tell of a pivotal event that took place a couple of days after our first visit to the Belgravia Gallery

Very early one morning Burke & Wills Removals and Storage in Camden London town was where three large goods wagons being pulled by Clydesdale's horses had been witnessed one morning by a mill worker while on his way home after his shift.

He (the mill worker had noticed that a large number of wooden crates were being taken off the goods wagons by two men (one at each end) and brought into the ware house for apparent storage. Other than noticing the odd hour of the delivery, and the number of goods wagons located there the man gave no thought to the early morning scene and continued on his way home.

If anyone had placed Burke & Wills Removals and Storage under continued surveillance they would have noticed several skilled tradesmen, with the tools of their profession entering early in the morning and leaving late at night for a period of about a week.

After hearing expert testimony as to why the Hughes painting was a forgery Holmes asked the young restorer "with what you have discovered about the oil paints that have been used to create this copy of the Long Engagement could you tell me by whom and where they were manufactured?'

"I'm not a chemist Mr. Holmes, but I have worked with pigments and oil paints long enough to tell you the basic materials that go into the manufacture of each color and from there I'm able to tell you who the company was who made each tube of paint. Leave this with me and I should have an answer for you within a couple of days."

On our ride back to 221 B Baker street Holmes said as much to himself as to me "This is a curious state Watson, an art forger who has not thought through the crime well enough by duplicating the oil paints used on the original making it less likely that if the copy was well executed it might not be detected as being a forgery."

A curious state indeed as we were to find out later that young Daniels, the art restorer was at a complete loss at identifying the components that made the oil paint used for the Hughes copy.

In the work area at the Belgravia Gallery standing next to the forged copy of The Long Engagement he stated "Gentlemen in all my years as an art restorer I have used and worked with many different types and kinds of pigments and oil paints, but there is nothing in these paints used that I can even come close to identifying."

Even more curious was the fact that suddenly more forgeries with the unidentifiable oil paints were starting to show up at the Belgravia Gallery as well as other reputable galleries in the greater London area.

Chapter 16

The next morning as we were finishing breakfast Holmes, sitting on the other side of the breakfast table stated to himself as much as to me "This will not do." "Do what?" I returned while putting down my cup hoping to catch the thread of his thought.

Holmes answered "Art forgeries that cannot be traced, reasonably good reproductions being produced with an unknown type of oil paint" "Where do you suggest that we start then?" I asked encouragingly. "By paying a visit to some one who may possibly be connected to this affair in ways we may have overlooked." Curious to know who this mysterious person was I asked "Who could it be?"

Holmes answer and line of reason I found hard to believe but after he finished he ended his reasoning with "When Watson you have eliminated all which is impossible, then whatever remains, however improbable, must be the truth." Holmes then announced he would be out for the rest of the day but when he returned he might be a step closer to solving the mystery.

Later that afternoon a bedraggled criminal looking fellow was seen entering the Rookery then making his way slowly along to the Old Mint located along the Ratcliffe Highway and Petticoat lane. Black John, as the fellow introduced himself in a gruff voice to the proprietor of the Old Mint asked if he could speak with Montague John Druitt.

"Druitt?" the proprietor answered Black John questioningly as if he had no knowledge of the person and if he did he didn't want to reveal that he might know him to the ruffian that was standing in front of him.

"The lodger who has or had rooms upstairs in this establishment!" answered Black John impatiently. Then as the bedraggled criminal waited for a reply he slowly started metamorphosing into my friend Sherlock Holmes.

Holmes reputation was well known in this part of London and when the transformation was almost complete the proprietor suddenly realized who he was facing his knowledge of Druitt's where about came back to him.

"Mr. Druitt moved out some time ago, he mentioned that he was going abroad to the continent for a time to talk to some people about an idea he recently had in mind. "I only have two more questions to ask" Holmes continued as he shed the last vestiges of Black John.

"One, at any time was a lady seen entering and leaving his residence?" "Yes" was the proprietor's quick answer. "And why I remember seeing her was that she was uncomfortably carrying what looked like a large roll of paper when she arrived, but didn't have it with her when she left."

"Two" Holmes told me later that he didn't want to ask this question but felt compelled to "When Druitt left for his trip to the continent, was there anything unusual about his luggage?" "Well yes sir" the proprietor had answered "besides a couple of cases and a steamer trunk he appeared to be carrying a similarly large roll of paper with him like the one the one the lady had left before.

Holmes finished his investigation by asking to see where Druitt had resided. "Well there isn't much to see besides the furniture; Mr. Druitt packed all his personal belongings along with some oil paintings I assumed he owned before he left.

Holmes pressed with his request and was lead up a flight of old and creaky wooden stairs to where Druitt had conducted his criminal business. As had been described the dingy rooms were bereft of any personal goods except for the few pieces of bare furniture that came with the weekly rent.

Holmes assuring the proprietor he would properly close the door when he left he excused him then began a closer examination of Druitt's last whereabouts. The only indication as to the level of Druitt's criminal activity was the large number of exposed nails that had been driven into the walls indicating that a variety of pictures or paintings may have hung there just a short while ago.

Holmes scoured cupboards, drawers, table top, the bed and closets to find that Druitt had not left anything of his inhabitance behind. Out of habit Holmes gave the floor a quick look not expecting to see any thing when his attention was attracted to a small cylindrical object lying almost neglected next to the empty coal stove.

Walking over to it he bent down and picked up the object examined it closely and sniffed it "Aha!" he exclaimed with joy while putting the hard won prize into a vest pocket for safe keeping "Now I have you Druitt" When Holmes made his entrance through the front door of his rooms later I put my journal down and asked

"Did you manage to talk to Druitt?" "No" was his answer, "and if it wasn't for this" at which time he pulled out of his vest pocket what looked very much like the remains of a cigarette "there would be no evidence at all that Druitt had ever occupied the rooms I looked through."

Removing his top hat and coat Holmes continued "and my worst fears have been confirmed Watson. Our Mr. Druitt has gone abroad to conduct some business with people who have are experts in machinery and electricity." "That in and of its self shouldn't be cause for too much concern" I countered.

"Watson do you remember our conversation with Mr. Wells and his shocking revelation" "Vaguely yes" I replied still trying to see the gravity of what Holmes had found out.

"Remember his words Watson"....*I have not been entirely truthful with both of you on that matter.*" remember my asking him *how so?* Then remember that he looked almost relieved when he said I *have long thought that it might be possible, in theory at least to have a set of mechanical drawings that could again in theory describe how to build my time machine. My machine is now one step beyond fiction, theory and imagination gentlemen. I now own a set of mechanical drawings, that with the right materials, skills and abilities it could be built.*"

I felt as if the floor had opened up when Holmes finished with "and the proprietor of the Old Mill where Druitt had rooms this after noon told me when I asked about Druitt's luggage *"Well yes sir, besides a couple of cases and a steamer trunk he appeared to be carrying a similarly large roll of paper with him like the one the one the lady had left before.*

"I think Watson it would be in our best interests to make discreet inquiries with the booking agents to see if they have seen anyone of Druitt's description and if they have if they can enlighten us as to where his destinations were when he was expected to arrive on the continent."

Holmes walked over his parlor windows that over looked Baker Street watched the late afternoon parade of humanity and industry for a short time, then turned to me and announced "Watson we shall have to ask Mr. Wells to come and visit us again and give us a full and complete disclosure of what he truly knows of this matter."

Chapter 17

When H.G. Wells walked through the front door of Holmes rooms the next afternoon the atmosphere was much more subdued. Hanging up his hat and coat Wells announced "Dr. Watson I was surprised to get your note and got here as quickly as I could." As we were all sitting down I expected Homes to share his news about Druitt with Wells instead

Holmes went straight into what concerned him the most. "I must ask you Mr. Wells is your time machine only a theory or is it possible to construct one?" "Mr. Holmes, when I wrote this story there is much I left out." "The relevant details being?" queried Holmes. "That time travel is possible and how the machine makes it happen.

But you have to understand this kind of knowledge in the wrong hands could be dangerous." "When I had the mechanical drawings executed it was only to prove that the machine could be constructed and could operate in the way I described in my story."

"A moot point Mr. Wells, it appears that some one has come into possession of this information by way of a duplicate copy of the mechanical drawings and may make your theoretical," Holmes waved his hand in Mr. Well's direction, "machine a reality."

"I can only speculate as to what type of havoc such a machine might be capable of doing, but because I have knowledge of the person who has the drawings so we can rule out any major crime like bank robbery happening once the machine becomes operational."

Wells now looking a little sheepish asked "Do you know who has the copy of the mechanical drawings and how they came into possession of it?" "The who Mr. Wells, is one Montague John Druitt,"

"Watson can testify that Druitt was considered by many to be the number one suspect in the Jack the Ripper case how ever there was very little evidence with which to implicate him. He has been incarcerated for the theft of small to medium sized oil paintings and was also in the business of creating reasonably good forgeries of the stolen paintings to sell to less than discriminate buyers."

"I have a feeling that Druitt is going to find a use for your machine that the character in your story never thought of or much less imagined. As to the how I can't really tell you, however I have it on good evidence that recently a lady was seen in Druitt's company and the she was see carrying what looked like a large roll of papers no doubt unlike a set of mechanical drawings."

From the look of dismay and regret that was playing across Wells face I reasoned that he knew who in fact the lady was and why she had done this. Then realizing the gravity of what had been set in motion Wells stated "Mr. Holmes we will have to prevent this Druitt character from doing any harm at any cost." Reflecting back to events that had taken place at the Belgravia Gallery and to the conversations we had both had with the managing director and the art restorer Holmes very matter of fact stated "I think Mr. Wells that with what I have ascertained from a reputable art gallery here in London Druitt may have already put his plan into motion."

Looking very puzzled Wells asked Holmes "How do you know this?" Before answering Holmes looked to me for some guidance. I minimally shook my head to him conveying that the less Wells knew at this time the better.

Taking my cue as he stood up and helped Wells to his feet, "Watson if you would be so kind as to fetch Mr. Wells's hat and coat." Putting on his coat and hat Wells no doubt felt a little like he had been suddenly been left out in the cold, Holmes placed his hand reassuringly upon Wells shoulder and said to him "Rest assured Mr. Wells that when we know more about this matter we shall be in touch with you."

Holmes saw to it that I escort our guest down the flight of carpeted stairs from Holmes rooms to the front door. As we were both standing in the door way waiting for Wells hansom cab to arrive I told him that as a married man I had a pretty good idea of how events had come to this stage. That Druitt would be stopped one way or another and that with some luck Wells name and reputation would never come to any type of harm.

Chapter 18

While climbing back up the carpeted stairs to Holmes late
afternoon lit parlor I had a chance to think about what he
had alluded to with Wells. Seeing Holmes seated with his
head casually buried in the paper...realizing he wasn't really
reading but only waiting for me to ask the obvious
question.

"Holmes" I started "are you seriously considering the fact
that not only does Druitt have a working time machine, but
that he is somehow employing it to make fairly good
forgeries." "If so" I continued "that would mean that he has
the ability to travel back and forth in time."

I was waiting for my friend to put the paper down and
break out in raucous laughter revealing that he had played
some elaborate joke on me. "Not back in time Watson but
forward" I could tell by the seriousness of his look that this
was not some joke after all.

"But how can you be sure?" I asked suddenly feeling the
need to be seated. "Up until recently I had a number of
separate of leads I could have followed that might have lead
to finding out where these mysterious paintings have come
from."

One by one Holmes listed them "One" he said as he raised
the first long finger of his hand..."Druitt being at the lecture
then after questioning Wells about his at the time
theoretical machine...two" and up went a second finger

"Mr. Wells confiding in us that he had...again at the time a set of mechanical drawings for his machine"

"Three" and the ring finger of his hand went up "the sudden appearance of the forgeries which at the beginning may have had nothing to do with Druitt having a time machine, but with more and more painting showing up proves that he does have use of a time machine now."

"Four" and all of the digits of his hand were up "the ex Mrs. Wells being seen in the company of Druitt and the apparent exchange of a copy of the mechanical drawing for a...what I would think was a considerable sum of money."

Five" and with that all five digits of his hand were up and as if to prove his point he spread all five out slightly "here is where all the previous facts are connected to this last one Druitt suddenly taking leave of his lodgings for a trip to the continent. Along with the usual luggage he was seen carrying a very large roll of paper...which we fatefully have to assume Watson was copy of Wells mechanical drawings for his machine."

"Well I certainly agree with you Holmes and Wells that Druitt has to be stopped before he does irreparable damage to the art world, but even given that he is using a machine of some size how do we begin to locate him, let alone stop him?"

Here Holmes gave me a smile of some confidence "with the help of the Baker Street Irregulars" he answered. Here I must stop and explain who Holmes had just made reference to.

Chapter 19

About five years ago Holmes had been asked to help solve a rash of shop lifting and pick pocketing. The fact that the Metropolitan Police could not find any clues or even suspects to these crimes they had asked Holmes to bring his powers of reason and deduction into play to halt this disturbing trend.

Holmes had learned a very long time ago that to catch a criminal you have to think like one a look like one. It didn't take too long in disguise to find out there was a band of young boys, who through sheer financial and social necessity had been forced to turn to a life of petty crime.

When they were apprehended by Holmes and he realized they were not hardened criminals Holmes seeing an opportunity offered them a much more pleasant alternative to prison or the work house. I remember Holmes telling me of the moment the Baker Street Irregulars coming into existence.

Standing among the boys Holmes offered them a future. His exact words to them were "Gentlemen a consulting detective such as myself can only be in one place at any time. I need to have eyes and ears everywhere to watch and report on criminals and any criminal behavior.

The number of and the average age of the Baker Street Irregulars depended on the financial situation each of the boys found themselves in. At its smallest there were only about five boys aged from ten to fifteen years of age. At its largest there could be as many as twenty boys aged from ten to seventeen years of age.

The unofficial leader of the Baker Street Irregulars at this time was a lad called Peter Stockton. "Watson" Holmes directed me "make arrangements through my usual means that Peter is contacted and comes to 221 Baker Street as soon as he can. We have no time to lose."

When Peter was in our company Holmes gave him a newspaper picture of Druitt with instructions that the Baker Street Irregulars were not to approach him or have any contact with, but were to come back to Holmes or myself if they had any knowledge of Druitt's location.

With Holmes extended eyes and ears now roaming the streets of London I hoped that Druitt would soon be spotted. Each afternoon one of us would rise from where we were seated in Holmes parlor in hopes of seeing a young lad come to the front door telling us our quarry had been spotted.

Holmes was about to give up with his method of finding Druitt and formally hand the matter over to the Metropolitan Police when we heard a soft knocking downstairs late one afternoon on the front door and Mrs. Hudson's voice answering the knock with "coming ."

We heard the door open there was a brief exchange of words then we heard her say "Up the stairs and knock before entering." We noticed that the carpeted stairs were barely being tread on as they were being ascended which left us wondering as to the nature of our caller and the urgency of the information they were bearing

This time we heard the knock on Holmes front door "Come in" was Holmes answer as we both rose to greet our afternoon visitor. Expecting to see some slight built man or women come through the door instead our visitor was a ten year old boy named Tom who was part of Holmes Baker Street Irregulars.

The boy removed his cap and went straight into his message "Mr. Holmes we (of course meaning some of the other members of the Baker Street Irregulars as well) think we have seen the man you have been looking for."

Ignoring me for a moment Holmes lowered his form down to the lads' level and asked excitedly "Where did you see him?" "Well sir" young Tom said as if to correct himself "we saw a man who looked like him and he was seen driving a team of Clydesdale horses pulling a large pulling a large wagon on Garret lane.

"What time was this?" Holmes asked the lad with the same enthusiasm a blood hound has when it picks up the scent of the prey. "Well it was early...about five o'clock in the morning or so we wanted to get to the bakery in time to see if they had any day old bread to give away"

Holmes cringed slightly when hearing about such needless poverty and I knew because of this that the Baker Street Irregulars would be paid well for this important lead.

When he straightened again he went to the mantle where he kept a loose collection of coins, scooping them up he placed the collection in Toms small hands. Looking at the bounty that he just received all the lad could muster was "thank you".

"This reward is for you and the rest of the Irregulars for your excellent work. When you get back instruct Peter and the rest to continue to keep the man you have seen under continued surveillance. You are not to let him know he is being watched, but let me know if you have information as to his where about and any further activities."

Chapter 20

When Tom had left to bring back the bounty he had received to the rest of the Baker Street Irregulars Holmes asked me "Watson what do we know about the area surrounding Garrett Lane and summers town Road in Camden town."

I had to think a moment then remembering some of the work injury related patients who had come into hospital from that area. Closing my eyes and seeing the patients being off loaded by stretcher bearers from the ambulances and being taken into the hospital for care I recited from memory "shops, tanneries maybe an iron foundry and a few ware houses.

With that last bit of information Holmes eyes just lit up then with the joy any criminal might have when picking and opening a particularly challenging lock. In a broad gesture of his hands he asked me "Watson where would be the best place to store and operate a time machine from?" Hoping I was on the same trail that he was I guessed "A ware house?"

"Indeed...not only is it a convenient place to hide the machine and keep it away from prying eyes but also a very convenient and practical place to store original and forged works of art.

Over the next several days Holmes and I visited each the ware houses located in the area surrounding Garrett Lane and Summers town Road. Each in turn was removed from the list of possible hiding places because they were either occupied in some way, were too small and not suitable or were in a bad state of repair.

Except for the few which were employed and exhibited clues of their function, such as horse shoe prints and wagon wheel tracks most looked like they had not seen any use in sometime..

Chapter 21

It was our last place to visit that both Holmes and myself hoped our fortune would change. Burke & Wills Removals and Storage (proclaimed the faded ornate red letters painted across a pair of wide wooden vertically hung folding doors) had been located at the junction of Garrett Lane and Summers town Road in Camden town for some time.

When we first walked around we thought because of its state it too had been abandoned, it was Homes that first noticed that it was still in use. "Look Watson faint horse shoe and wagon wheel tracks leading into the ware house."

I admit when I looked at the clues Holmes was pointing to I couldn't see any evidence, but when I shifted slightly to the right I could see what Holmes had spied.

"Now Watson it's time to find out who is making use of this ware house and why." "I see there is an workman's entrance set in one of the vertical doors" knowing that I did not like to step out side the law he assured me "if you wish to remain outside while I enter you can keep watch and let me know if any one approaches."

But knowing I was as curious as he was as to what might be inside I followed after him. Our progress to enter was only momentarily halted by the fact that the entry door was pad locked. Not even bothered by this inconvenience Holmes reached into one of his inner pockets of his coat and produced a set of fine set of lock picking tools

Chapter 22

I should pause here for a moment to let the reader know
that I found some of Holmes actions to be wrong such as
his willingness to bend the truth and break the law (such as
lie to the police, conceal evidence, burgle and house break)
when it suited his purposes.

In these (Victorian) times, such actions were not
necessarily considered vices as long as they were done by a
gentleman for noble purposes, such as preserving a
woman's honor or a family's reputation, or bringing a man
like Montague John Druitt to justice.

I watched in fascination as Holmes manipulated the two
fine picks inside the lock then watched and heard as the
hasp dropped away from the body of the lock. We removed
the lock, opened the door and quickly made our way into
the ware house.

There was just enough light coming in from the over head
weather stained sky lights which meant Holmes and I
would not have unnecessarily attract any attention to our
business by lighting a coal oil lamp.

As we walked around about the only things we observed
would be the same sorts of things that would be seen in
other ware houses. There were small and large wooden
packing crates every where some by them selves and others
stacked on top and beside each other. We had walked all

around the perimeter of the building and now found ourselves some where in the middle.

I was beginning to think we had lost our last hope and was ready to share this thought with Holmes when he asked me a curious question "Watson do you happen to notice anything in particular about where we are standing right now?" The only obvious observation I could make was that we were standing on a packed earth floor.

Then pointing all around he said "It is an odd thing that this ware house has packing crates of all manner and description stored everywhere but look at the size of the area we are standing is bereft of crates."

When Holmes paced out the dimensions of the area in question it was roughly about five feet in width and about fifteen feet in length. "You don't suppose?" I started then crouching down Holmes lightly touched what look like to be the impressions of two long pieces of pipe about five feet apart. Holmes looked up at me and replied "I believe it is."

Still not ready to accept the fact we had found evidence of the time machine I tried to make reason of what Holmes had found by saying that the impressions were nothing more than the results of two long lengths of pipe that had been stored there for some time.

Holmes now himself a little doubtful about the apparent evidence got up and went to where the back or front of the machine would be bent down and dusted for what I thought were more impressions of the machines existence.

Getting up again then coming back to me he said a well proven statement "Watson again when you have eliminated all which is impossible, then whatever remains, however improbable, must be the truth."

"We have found where Wells time machine is being operated from," as if to back up this incredible find Holmes then produced yet another discarded cigarette from the packed earth floor with the flair of a sleight of hand artist "this I believe will be prove to be the same brand of cigarette I found in Druitt's rooms if it matches the one I already have then all that will be left is for us is to apprehend the man who has lit and smoked both cigarettes.

Leaving the ware house and locking the workman's entrance then walking back to where we could find a hansom cab Holmes and I starting making plans to go back to the ware house very early the next morning and wait for Druitt's return.

Chapter 23

Returning to 221 B Baker Street Holmes instructed me as to what we would need for tomorrows early vigil while he conducted scientific tests on the two discarded cigarettes that were in his keep.

"Our Druitt is a man of expensive tastes Watson" came Holmes voice from his laboratory "How so?" was my reply while checking the coal oil lamp. "Both cigarettes are labeled as Dunbar it is an extraordinary cross-cut English flake the result of a complex mixture of the finest Virginias, choice Turkish and Oriental tobaccos hard-pressed and broad-cut into thick flakes."

"Where would Druitt have purchased them?" I asked my curiosity now piqued "An educated guess" my friend said. I already knew that he had fixed the shop where they had come from "J.F. Germain & Son pipe, cigarette tobaccos." was Holmes answer. A visit later that day to that particular tobacconist would confirm both the product and its customer.

Chapter 24

During my bachelor day with Holmes I remembered be awakened early in the morning to pursue some clue or apprehend some criminal but these early risings had always happened just as the sun was lighting the eastern sky. This particular morning as I was feeling myself being gently jostled and Holmes telling me wake and get ready to go it was still dark outside.

Sitting up on Holmes chesterfield shaking off the effects of sleep I asked the obvious question "What time of the night is it Holmes?" "It's three in the morning Watson, and to answer your next question I want us to be waiting at Burke & Wills Removals and Storage before Druitt arrives.

It was an odd site as we both quietly stepped out the front door of 221 B Baker Street to know that only Holmes, myself and the hansom cab driver were the only ones awake and active at this early hour.

"Watson you first" as he pointed towards the interior of the cab I listened from inside as Holmes first gave directions to the driver as to our destination then instructions to pick up other fares later that morning.

We arrived just before four in the morning and as the last time the pad lock on the entry door proved to be no challenge. Closing the entry door behind us and once inside the ware house Holmes lit the coal oil lamp so we could find our way around in the pitch dark interior.

Walking around carefully Holmes stated to me "Watson we will need some sort of blind where we can see the area where the machines tracks were found but where you and I cannot be detected."

Noticing a large collection of crates that were just a little more than waste high and wide enough for us not too be seen I pointed this "blind" out to Holmes. Going around Holmes and I crouched down and waited for Druitt's arrival. "Watson" Holmes asked did you bring your service revolver?" "I have a feeling that once Druitt has been found out he may not be too cooperative and may try to attempt an escape."

I opened my coat just enough for Holmes to see the weapon. Pulling out his pocket watch from his vest and seeing what time it was Holmes extinguished the coal oil lamp and announced "I believe Druitt will be joining us shortly

Still finding the thought of a functioning time machine hard to believe and accept I fully expected the large vertical doors to start opening shortly and see a team of horses pulling a large goods wagon start to make its way inside.

Chapter 25

What we both witnessed next had never been seen by any one before except by the characters in Wells novel and after today would never be witnessed again. It as if one fire fly had some how gotten into the darkened ware house only to be joined by more and more. These insects seemed to bringing with them the energy one feels just before a lighting storm

They swirled around loosely for a short time then the different point of lights started to coalesce into a single source of light. It was at this point I expected to see and a feel a lightening bolt the bright light remained formless only for a short time then started to take shape.

Looking just over top of the crates at the phenomenon I asked Holmes "Is that Wells time machine?" My question was answered as the image of light started to take on more color and form.

I should say here that to truly appreciate this event the reader would have had to have been present with us that morning to witness this event. Words make a poor substitute but I shall try to tell you what I saw next.

Even before it came into final focus I could tell that the machine was constructed of brass tubes or rails. Even with out measuring it I tell it was the length and width we had determined from our last visit.

Not a lot of fine detail of the machine was still visible except for two facts, one I could just make out that there was some one (I assumed it was Druitt) operating the machines controls and two there was a large disk at the rear of the machine was seemed to slowing down while still rotating.

Still just looking over the top of the crate we saw the large disk almost stop its motion it was then that we knew we had our quarry. In front of us with out any doubt was Wells time machine. The mechanical drawings didn't give any real credit or justice as to what a piece of engineering it was or what a work of art it was.

As I had ascertained it was Druitt seated at the controls from what I could tell he was pushing down on a small crystal shaft obviously to stop the machine. Still mesmerized by this wonder I heard Holmes instruct me "Now is the moment Watson. Draw your service revolver." Then we both reveled ourselves to Druitt from behind the crates where we had been hidden.

Surprised that Druitt hadn't seen our motion Holmes announced to him in a loud voice "Druitt remove you hands from the machines controls and place them in the air!" Looking both shocked and surprised Druitt failed to immediately react to Holmes instructions.

"Druitt" Holmes tried again "My friend Dr. Watson has a service revolver aimed at you and I should remind you that all his years in the army he has never missed his target." With that Druitt placed both his hands in the air and awaited further instructions.

"Now you will slowly stand up, remove yourself from the machine and walk slowly in our direction." Coming towards us in slow measured steps Druitt commented "Mr. Holmes and Dr. Watson, what a pleasure to see you both again. I had counted on us never crossing paths after the Jack the Ripper business."

"Well if not for at first glance a series of seemingly unconnected incidents we might not find ourselves here in this ware house at this early hour of the morning." Holmes returned.

"Watson, keep your service revolver pointed at Druitt while I go to investigate the extent of the damage he may have already done to the art world." With that both Druitt and I watched Holmes approach the time machine.

Chapter 26

First he stepped onto the machine and sat down on the chair Druitt had occupied upon his most spectacular arrival. Holmes then delicately touched all of the controls in front of him wisely understanding that he did not know their function or what might happen if he activated any of them.

He then turned around to notice a small collection of oil paintings that had been secured to the back of the operator's seat. Untying the cord that had held them there, he looked in turn to each one then looked directly at Druitt asking "Originals or copies?"

Druitt answered some what cryptically "Mr. Holmes in front of you there is a panel with two dates, one is my departure date and one is my arrival date. Read the date on the left then the one on the right that should answer your question.

Carefully putting the paintings back down Holmes turned around and followed Druitt's instructions. I held my breath while I waited to hear Holmes answer. I could tell he was having problems with the evidence the two panels were now presenting him with.

Then coldly and logically Holmes stated the date 1895 then followed with the date 1995. Already sensing my disbelief Druitt calmly said "Yes Dr. Watson with this remarkable machine I have traveled 100 years into the future. After I had it shipped from the continent and assembled here I wasn't too sure just how much potential it might have or be capable of. So my first few voyages were limited first to just a day then week, I thought of these early trips as voyages of exploration.

"Part of these early voyages of exploration was to see what this part of the city would look like in say a day or in year's time, but also to see if this particular ware house would still be here in whatever time I chose to travel to. It would make for very unnecessary complications to my plans for any one in the future to know about my machine and my uses for it. "

"When I was confident enough about my machines capabilities I went ahead 100 years. Fortune one hundred years in the future smiled on me Dr. Watson for although being a little worse for ware Burke & Wills Removals and Storage was still located here in 1995".

Chapter 27

I took umbrage that Druitt had referred to Wells machine as his own then commented on his bold and still some what unbelievable statement "Obviously with criminal intent" I muttered. Almost as if he had heard my comment or had read my thoughts Druitt continued "It wasn't too long before I realized the true potential of Mr. Wells's machine in connection to my profession."

"Art forgery in this time has reached a certain level of perfection, but there is the matter of how long it takes to produce a copy. I doubt that you are aware of the fact that creating a reasonable copy is a time consuming process, and for me anyway Dr. Watson volume is my prime consideration."

Despite the fact that I still had my service revolver pointed at him I could hear the sound of Druitt's voice get a bit cocky as if he was proud of what he had accomplished. I cut him off sharply by saying "How is the time machine connected with the forgeries."

Then before he began again a cold feeling ran down me when I remembered what Jeffery Daniels the young art restorer had told us about the forged Hughes painting *"Gentlemen in all my years as an art restorer I have used and worked with many different types and kinds of pigments and oil paints, but there is nothing in these paints used that I can even come close to identifying."*

Then in a moment of inspiration I deduced "You went far enough ahead in time to where you could locate resources and art forgers not unlike yourself to have copies that could be produced fairly quickly then brought back to this time to sell." Druitt acknowledged my observation with "You would be surprised Dr. Watson how fast a good copy of a painting such as, say The Long Goodbye by Hughes can be produced in the year 1995. And more so the number of art forgers who in that time are willing to carry out such a lucrative enterprise."

Chapter 28

Then Holmes coming back from the time machine to where we were both standing continued on the trail. "It was a brilliant plan no doubt, but it came to an end when a young art restorer could not identify the composition of the pigments in the oils that were used to paint the forged Hughes.

"Having knowledge of your criminal career and the fact you had dealings with the ex Mrs. Wells and what she was willing to part with no doubt for a considerable amount of money it was only a matter of time when our paths would cross." There was a moment of silence when Holmes and I heard an authoritative knock on the entrance door.

Holmes then pulled out his watch from his vest pocket then announced "Ah right on time. That should be the Metropolitan Police for our art forger" "Watson would you please escort Druitt to the trades man door and into their custody. Having to explain where these forged paintings came from will be tricky enough but having to explain the existence of a functioning time machine might be next to impossible.

While I escorted Druitt out of the ware house and into the hands of the waiting Metropolitan Police Holmes went back to remove the forged paintings still located behind the operators seat and no doubt to decide the fate of Wells functioning time machine.

Having transferred custody, seeing Druitt was being placed in the police wagon and starting its return journey back towards its final destination I too starting have questions to about the fate of such an elegant and technological wonder.

Chapter 29

Walking back into the warehouse I saw my friend deep in study about how one went about traveling into the future. I stood quietly beside him until he was ready to share any observations he might have "It is almost miraculous how a set of mechanical drawing can become what we see before us isn't it Watson"

Asking the obvious "What's to done with it then?" "I think that should be decided by its creator who should be joining us shortly." Holmes answered." You have invited Wells here. You were very confident then that you would apprehend Druitt then" Holmes smiled the briefest of smiles then said   "You can...never foretell what any one man will do, but you can say with precision what an average number will be up to. Individuals vary, but percentages remain constant."

A softer knock on the entrance door told of us Wells arrival. "Watson if would be so kind as to let Mr. Wells in and prepare him for the inevitable shock he is about to experience." So as instructed I went to the entrance door opened it and invited Wells inside.

Chapter 30

"Good morning Dr. Watson I received a message from hansom cab driver to be here this morning and I was wondering what it was in regard to." "Mr. Wells" I started before we preceded any further "it is in regards to your time machine." "Do you mean that the second set of drawings has been recovered?" Wells questioned me.

"More than that" was all I could answer, "come with me please." As Wells and I made our way into the middle of the ware house he observed two sites, my friend Holmes standing next to for Wells at least a very real time machine.

At this point I could tell that Wells was very much at a loss for words while he beheld the site that was presented to him. Partial sentences were all he could manage "That's impossible...that can't...this isn't re..."

Holmes not wanting Wells to struggle with the reality of the situation said "Mr. Wells the machine you see before is quite real and fully functional." Wells being a man of logic questioned this fact by asking "How is this so?"

Holmes then went into a brief explanation of how Wells ex wife, a copy of the mechanical drawings, three inventors, an art forger by the name of Montague John Druitt and a time trip 100 years into the future almost ruined the art world had all made it so.

"100 years?" Wells asked with out fully understanding what he had just been told. "Mr. Wells if you would step over here" Holmes pointed in the general direction of the machines controls.

Wells joined my friend now standing in front of the machines controls much as Druitt had revealed the record of the machines travels Holmes now stated Mr. Wells "in front of you there is a panel with two dates, one is departure date and one is the arrival date. Read the date on the left then the one on the right that should answer your question."

Wells silently mouthed the two dates he saw "1895 – 1995" Giving Wells a few minutes to let this information settle in Holmes gravely stated "Seeing this, and knowing how such technology could be used for great good also for great evil it is very obvious that this machine should not be allowed to fall into the wrong hands."

Wells asked with almost the same type of voice that one asks upon learning about the death of a loved one "Are you suggesting that my time machine be destroyed?" This was one of the rare times when I have ever seen my friend at a loss for words.

I could see that there was some conflict going on in my Holmes mind about this matter. There was the fact that the machine was a technological wonder a marvel and a wonder of its time. But there was the matter that Druitt had used it for no good but his own.

Holmes no doubt realized that Druitt was for all purposes a small time criminal but if such a machine was to fall into the hands of an arch enemy like Professor Moriarty who knows what the outcome might be. .

Not being able to look at Wells growing sad face Holmes turned to me and stated "Watson we have a dilemma. It is obvious that with what has happened Mr. Well's creation cannot continue to exist, but it is almost unthinkable that this machine should be destroyed."

Chapter 31

For some reason I saw Druitt's hand on the small crystal rod pushing it down to make the machine stop. Sensing some solution to this problem I asked Wells "The small crystal shaft in front of operator. Pushing it down makes the machine stop and pushing it up makes if go...correct?"

Wells nodded his head in agreement. Then sensing where this was going he said "Once the machine has been stopped the crystal shaft can safely be removed thus making the machine inoperable until it has been reinserted"

Forming a workable solution in my head I looked around the immediate area until I spied a long length of heavy twine. "Mr. Wells I believe I have a solution to both yours and Holmes problem.

Gathering up the twine and taking it to the machine I asked Holmes, knowing his expertise about knots to wrap the crystal shaft a couple of times then securely tie the twine. "Mr. Wells how far into the future is your machine capable of traveling to?"

Until just now only experiencing his machine as a set of mechanical drawings Wells was unsure of the answer. Crouching down Wells scrutinized the controls until he found the one that would set the machines destination date.

"Well this is incredible Dr. Watson and Mr. Holmes but it appears who ever built the machine had in mind going far into the future." said Wells as he continued to appreciate the craftsmanship that had been involved in bringing the mechanical drawings to life.

Drawing Wells back to the present I asked again "How far? to the year 2295 Dr. Watson." "Watson" Holmes said with some pride as he figured out my compromise "you propose to send Mr. Wells machine far enough into the future where it will cause no harm or ever be accessible to anyone. Then Holmes smiled when he finished working out the last details "And thus saving it from being needlessly destroyed."

Holmes then turned to the one person who had the most to loose in these events "Is Dr. Watsons compromise agreeable with you Mr. Wells?" Wells looking considerably relieved nodded yes. Then with Wells setting the machines final arrival date all three of us left the machine with me paying the twine in front of us as we walked backward to about ten feet away from the machine.

Chapter 32

When I had reached the end of the twine I pulled it taught then handed it to Wells. "When you are ready" I said to Wells realizing he needed no instruction as to what to do next. Knowing what would happen as he pulled on the now much taught twine Wells looked first at me then at Holmes and hauntingly asked "Can I have one last look at my machine before I send it into oblivion?"

Holmes and I understanding that Wells had just come to accept that his very much theoretical had come into being and that none of us would ever see it again agreed to give him a little time alone to inspect and become aquatinted with the time machine.

We watched as the twine slipped from Wells fingers and he made his way over to where the machine was resting. When he got to it he caressed the shiny brass frame, stroked the polished wood work, and peered intently at the controls, instruments and the machinery that made it do what it was built to do but to both Holmes and my amazement he did not sit in the operator's seat.

Coming back to where Holmes and I were standing Wells picked up the end of the twine and announced "Gentlemen I am ready" We watched as Wells gave the twine a short but firm tug, the crystal rod in response moved up a bit and we the saw the large disk at the back of the machine start to rotate.

With each tug Wells applied to the twine the crystal rod moved further up and the faster the disk started to spin. Then in a reverse or what we had seen when the machine first had arrived arrive the image of the machine started to get more and more out of focus.

Chapter 33

It was at this time Holmes did something totally unexpected, he took the end of the twine from Wells fingers, gave it a sharp pull up as this was taking place two remarkable things happened first the machine winked out of existence and the crystal control rod now separated from its socket shot up towards the ceiling of the warehouse paused for the briefest time then fell and landed with a soft thud on the packed earth floor.

Wells looked both amazed and a little confused as to Holmes last minute action. Holmes taking the moment in stride said to Wells as he went over the pick up the crystal control rod. "Mr. Wells there has never been a machine like yours before and there will never be another like it again."

Then walking back with the crystal control rod in his hand Holmes presented it to Wells saying "A souvenir or a memento as it were to your genius Mr. Wells, save for your mechanical drawings you will never have the machine but you will have some small physical proof to yourself that a creation of your brilliant imagination came into being.

After sharing a handsome cab back into the city and first saying good bye then dropping off   Wells (with his souvenir) at his residence Holmes and I returned to 221 B Baker Street in time for a late breakfast. As were finishing the last of the coffee and the remainder of the toast we both heard Mrs. Hudson calling from downstairs that there was a message for me.

Holmes realizing it was probably from my wife asking me to come home said "you had better pack Watson; no doubt your wife is waiting for you at Paddington station with her luggage wanting you to escort her home."

With out waiting for Mrs. Hudson to deliver the message I asked as I was getting up from the breakfast table "How can you be sure?" A rare but genuine warm smile played out on Holmes face as he answered "This is one time when my brain is governed my heart. I may never have been in love but I know of love.

However Watson love is an emotional thing, and whatever is emotional is opposed to that true cold reason which I place above all things. I should never marry myself, lest I bias my judgment.

Dr. John H. Watson M.D.

Transcribed from his original case notes by Mr. Fred Thursfield

June 06, 2010

After reading the account of this affair the reader may wonder what was the eventual fate of the last collection of paintings Druitt had brought back from the future with Wells time machine.

Because neither Holmes nor I at the time could ever ascertain as to whether or not they were in fact the originals or very good forgeries it was decided to have paintings taken from Burke & Wills Removals and Storage back to Holmes rooms which would act both as safe temporary storage for the collection and as an impromptu art gallery to display them

After we had both personally enjoyed the company of the collection for a short time Holmes felt that each should now be returned to their proper owners. To that end he placed a small notice in each of the afternoon news papers to be published in the next edition that was to state that some "stolen" art work had been recently recovered (with the help of the Metropolitan Police) and the location as to where the art work could be reclaimed.

The duly published notice in each paper discreetly left out the incredible details as to where the paintings had actually been located and how they had eventually come to be recovered. The notice factually informed the interested reader that if positive ownership of the piece could be properly established while attending at 221B Baker Street each "stolen" painting would gladly be returned to its rightful owner.

I should comment that it was with some mixed emotions that as each of the stolen pieces of art left with the person or gallery who had owned it before the "theft" Holmes and I would never be sure if we were in fact returning an original painting or a well executed forgery back into an unsuspecting world. Holmes succinctly summed up my thoughts on this subject with "Let us hope Watson that none of the paintings we are returning over the next few days and weeks ever finds its way to the Belgravia Art Gallery and into the capable hands of Jeffery Daniels our forgery expert for any type of cleaning or restoration.

J.H.W.

While transcribing Dr. Watson's case notes for this story a very coincidental event took place. When the British Museum was conducting its annual inventory (September last year) of the large number of items it has in storage that (for one reason or another) are rarely displayed and seen by the general public. An untagged small clear crystal rod was discovered among the collection. It measured about nine inches in length, had the circumference of a small napkin ring, one end had been cut as if to be placed in a socket and the crystal rod would have easily fit inside a person's hand. When the extensive museum records were searched to establish an acquisition date and accurately describe the nature of the mysterious object no record could be located as to how or when the museum had acquired the crystal rod or even of its intended purpose or use.

F.C.T.

The Discarded Cigarette is written in the style of...

The Seven-Per-Cent Solution a 1974 novel by American writer Nicholas Meyer. It is written as a pastiche of a Sherlock Holmes adventure, and was adapted for the cinema in 1976. The novel's full title is The Seven-Per-Cent Solution: Being a Reprint from the Reminiscences of John H. Watson, M.D.

Published as a "lost manuscript" of the late Dr. John H. Watson, the book recounts Holmes' recovery from cocaine addiction (with the help of Sigmund Freud) and his subsequent prevention of a European war through the unraveling of a sinister kidnapping plot. It was followed by two other Holmes pastiches by Meyer, The West End Horror (1976) and The Canary Trainer (1993), neither of which has been adapted to film.

Pastiche

In this usage, a work is called *pastiche* if it is *cobbled together* in imitation of several original works. As the *Oxford English Dictionary* puts it, a pastiche in this sense is "a medley of various ingredients; a hotchpotch, farrago, jumble." These meaning accords with etymology: *pastiche* is the French version of the greco-Roman dish pastitsio or *pasticcio*, which designated a kind of pie made of many different ingredients.

Authors note:

With the exception of Sherlock Holmes, the Baker Street Irregulars, The unofficial leader of the Baker Street Irregulars Peter Stockton, Dr. John Watson, his wife Mary, Mrs. Hudson the house keeper of 221 B Baker Street, Jeffery Daniels the art restorer, (Universal Catalog of Books on Art) The Brice Art Museum Exhibition Catalog 1890 edition, Charles Henry Stephenson the managing director of the Belgravia Gallery, the Belgravia Gallery, the proprietor of the Old Mint, the master of ceremonies at the St. James theater, H.G. Wells lecture at the St. James Theater and any of the hansom cab drivers mentioned all of the other characters in this story were based on people who were living in the year 1895. All of the locations mentioned in the story except for the Belgravia Art Gallery also existed in the year 1895.

The Time Machine (the novel) written by H.G. Welles

Wells had considered the notion of time travel before, in an earlier (but less well-known) work titled *The Chronic Argonauts*. He had thought of using some of this material in a series of articles in the *Pall Mall Gazette*, until the publisher asked him if he could instead write a serial novel on the same theme; Wells readily agreed, and was paid £100 on its publication by Heinemann in 1895. The story was first published in serial form in the *New Review* through 1894 and 1895. The book is based on the Block Theory of the Universe, which is a notion that time is a fourth space dimension.

The story reflects Wells' own socialist political views and the contemporary angst about industrial relations. It is also influenced by Ray Lankester's theories about social degeneration. Other science fiction works of the period, including Edward Bellamy's *Looking Backward*, and the later *Metropolis*, dealt with similar themes.

The inspirations for the characters in this story of Sherlock Holmes and Dr. Watson are based on the British actors Jeremy Brett as Holmes, Edward Hardwick as Watson and the American actor Malcolm McDowell as H.G. Wells.

Other MX Sherlock Holmes Titles

Short Fiction Collections

The Lost Stories of Sherlock Holmes

Outstanding Mysteries of Sherlock Holmes

Novels

Shadowfall

Barefoot on Baker Street

Rendezvous at The Populaire (vs The Phantom)

I Will Find The Answer (vs Dr. Jekyll)

A Case of Witchcraft

The Sign of Fear, A Study In Crimson (the adventures of the female Sherlock Holmes)

Sherlock Holmes and The Affair In Transylvania

Modern Fiction

No Police Like Holmes

Murder in the Library

The Case of the Grave Accusation

www.mxpublishing.com

Other MX Sherlock Holmes Titles (continued..)

Historical / Non Fiction

Close To Holmes

Eliminate the Impossible

The Norwood Author [winner 2011 Howlett Literary Award]

A Chronology of Sir Arthur Conan Doyle

Sherlock Holmes, Conan Doyle and Devon

Biographies

Watson's Afghan Adventure

In Search of Dr Watson

Bertram Fletcher Robinson

Special Collections

Baker Street Beat

and many more.........

www.mxpublishing.com

THE
OUTSTANDING
MYSTERIES
OF
SHERLOCK HOLMES

WRITTEN & ILLUSTRATED BY
GERARD KELLY

www.ingramcontent.com/pod-product-compliance
Lightning Source LLC
Chambersburg PA
CBHW071333130626
46556CB00004B/1873